76863 June 07

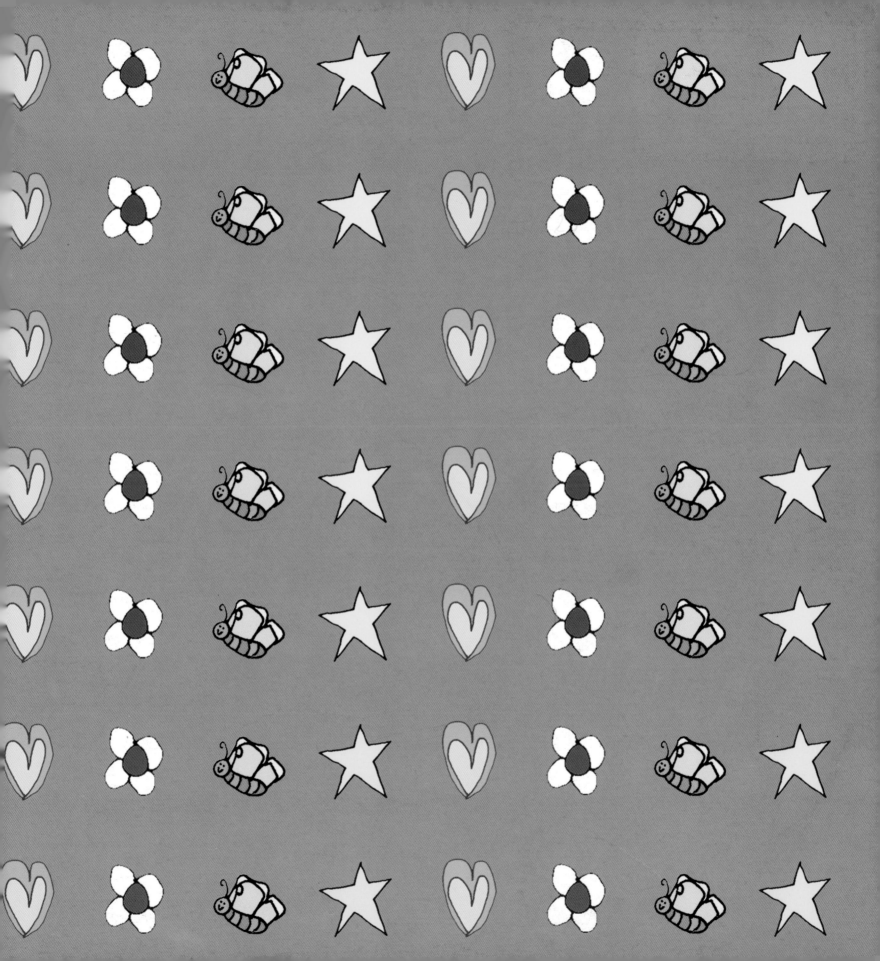

Licensed exclusively to Top That Publishing Ltd
Tide Mill Way, Woodbridge, Suffolk, IP12 1AP, UK
www.topthatpublishing.com
Copyright © 2014 Tide Mill Media
All rights reserved
0 2 4 6 8 9 7 5 3 1
Printed and bound in China

ISBN 978-1-78244-361-2

A catalogue record for this book is available from the British Library

The Tickle Misses

Party Pop

Alarm clocks ringing,
At the crack of dawn.
Hooray, it's party day!
Quick, get your clothes on!

Early at the edge of the forest
Jessie and Honey meet.
Honey has lots to do today.
She's in charge of special treats!

First thing in the morning
Is the best time to find dew.
They collect it from a spider's web.
For the perfect fairy brew!

It doesn't take them very long
To fill bottles to the top.
They put them in the wheelbarrow.
It will be such fizzy pop!

Now the fairies find fresh fruit
To add flavour to the punch.
Strawberries and cherries,
So fab with party lunch!

The bottles make the barrow heavy,
It's very hard to push.
Jessie wishes for her fairy wand.
Magic will make it whoosh!

Back at Honey's house,
They empty out the cart.
Later they'll make pink punch
For when the party starts.

Carefully they collect the cakes,
Gateaux, buns, and treats,
So delicious and so tempting,
So lip-lickingly sweet!

All the food is laid on the table.
It makes such a wonderful spread.
Honey wants to nibble and taste
But has to resist instead!

Finally, they get back home,
And have a little rest.
Then Honey gets a huge tub out
In which the berries will be pressed.

They tie their skirts into knots
To keep their dresses neat.
Then into the tub, so slippy,
Berries squelching beneath their feet!

Oh dear! Poor Jessie's fallen!
Splat! Into the tub.
That fruit juice is so messy.
She's going to need a good scrub!

Ha ha! Look at Honey!
In that red polka-dot dress.
Of course Honey's not upset
But oh dear. What a mess!

Time to add the fizzy water
And stir the mixture up.
A little taste ... it's yummy!
But Jessie starts to hiccup!

Now the punch is all finished.
Back in the bottles it goes.
Then out to Jessie's tables.
The stars are starting to glow.

Nearly party time at last!
The fairy friends say goodbye.
They go home to get beautiful,
So excited as they fly.

Jessie's bath is piled with bubbles
Right up to the brim.
Look at the lather turning red,
As the berry juice comes off her skin.

Yippee! Time to get ready.
I wonder what Jessie will choose?
A favourite dress, in perfect pink,
Stripy tights and dancing shoes!

First to arrive are Jessie's best friends,
All of the Tickle Misses!
Dressed in their best, so sparkly,
And full of good party wishes.

Next to arrive, it's Mr. Snail
Wearing his colourful shell.
What's that light behind him?
Oh, here come the glow-worms as well.

Lots more guests have arrived
Dressed up and ready to play.
They all bring gifts of food and drink,
All ready to party away!

Jessie, who's the perfect host
Checks everyone's having fun.
What a super, spectacular time.
The night has just begun!

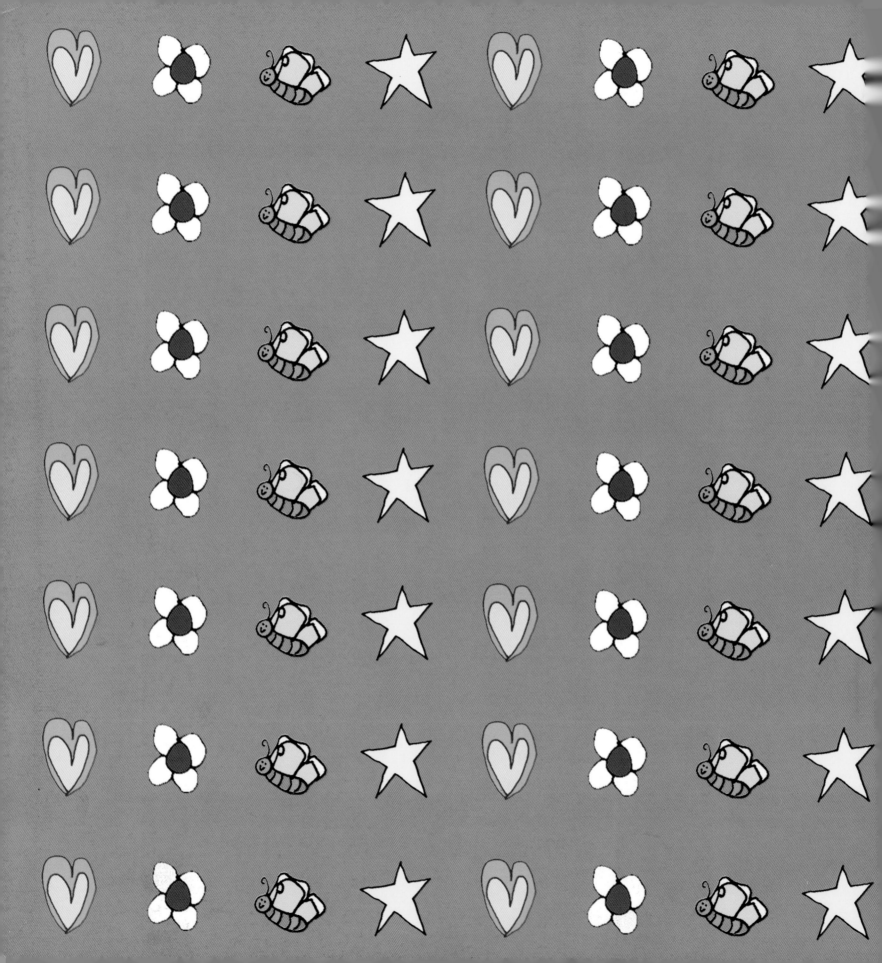

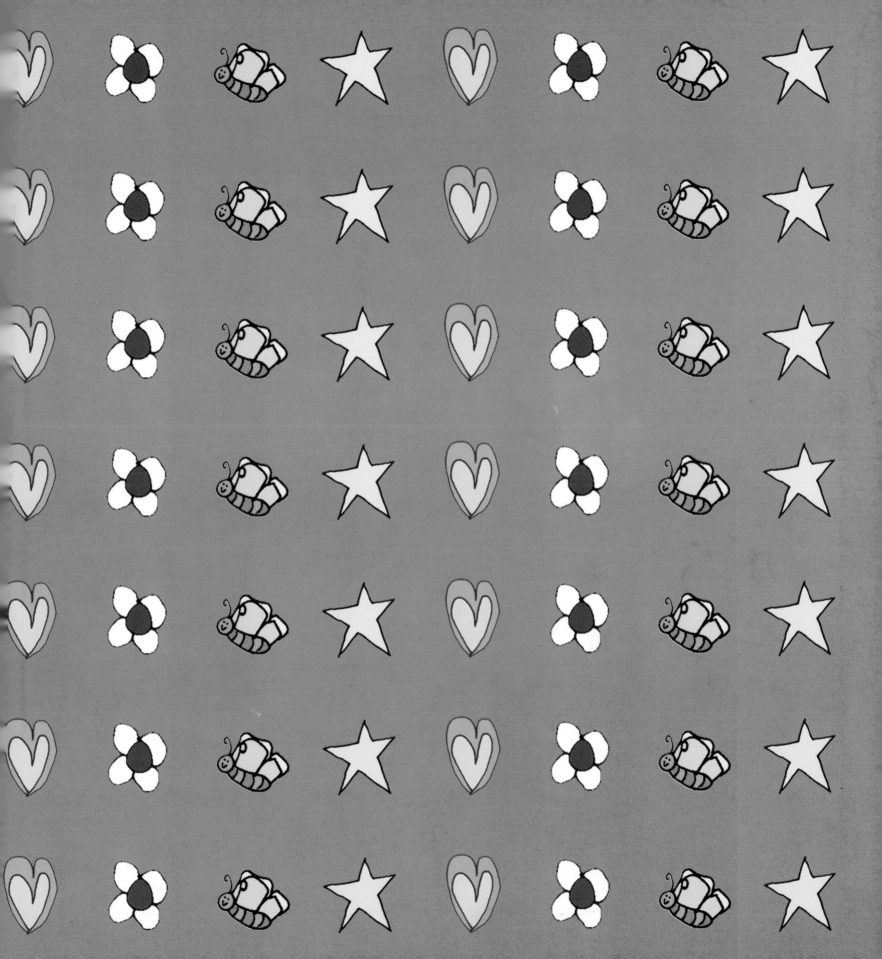

Look Out!

If you liked Party Pop,
try these other great Tickle Misses titles:

ISBN 978-1-78244-360-5

ISBN 978-1-78244-359-9

ISBN 978-1-78244-362-9

Poppy

Sparkle

The
Tickle
Misses

Honey

Jessie